A NOTE TO PARENTS

When your children are ready to "step into reading," giving them the right books—and lots of them—is as crucial as giving them the right food to eat. **Step into Reading Books** present exciting stories and information reinforced with lively, colorful illustrations that make learning to read fun, satisfying, and worthwhile. They are priced so that acquiring an entire library of them is affordable. And they are beginning readers with an important difference—they're written on four levels.

Step 1 Books, with their very large type and extremely simple vocabulary, have been created for the very youngest readers. **Step 2 Books** are both longer and slightly more difficult. **Step 3 Books,** written to mid-second-grade reading levels, are for the child who has acquired even greater reading skills. **Step 4 Books** offer exciting nonfiction for the increasingly proficient reader.

Children develop at different ages. **Step into Reading Books,** with their four levels of reading, are designed to help children become good—and interested—readers *faster*. The grade levels assigned to the four steps—preschool through grade 1 for Step 1, grades 1 through 3 for Step 2, grades 2 and 3 for Step 3, and grades 2 through 4 for Step 4—are intended only as guides. Some children move through all four steps very rapidly; others climb the steps over a period of several years. These books will help your child "step into reading" in style!

Copyright © 1984 Children's Television Workshop. MUPPET Characters © 1984 Muppets Inc. All rights reserved under International and Pan-American Copyright Conventions. ® Sesame Street and the Sesame Street sign are trademarks and service marks of the Children's Television Workshop. Published in the United States by Random House, Inc., New York, and simultaneously in Canada by Random House of Canada Limited, Toronto, in conjunction with the Children's Television Workshop.

Library of Congress Cataloging in Publication Data:
Lerner, Sharon. Big Bird's copycat day. (Step into reading. A Step 1 book) SUMMARY: Big Bird enjoys spending the day doing whatever he sees anyone else doing, whether wagging his tail like a dog or being grouchy like Oscar. [1. Puppets—Fiction. 2. Imitation—Fiction. 3. Stories in rhyme] I. Mathieu, Joe, ill. II. Children's Television Workshop. III. Title.   PZ8.3.L5493Bi 1984 [E]   84-6869   ISBN: 0-394-86912-5 (trade); 0-394-96912-X (lib. bdg.)

Manufactured in the United States of America   26 27 28 29 30

STEP INTO READING is a trademark of Random House, Inc.

Step into Reading™

Big Bird's Copycat Day

Featuring Jim Henson's Sesame Street Muppets

by Sharon Lerner
illustrated by Joe Mathieu

A Step 1 Book

Random House/Children's Television Workshop

I like to be a copycat.

I copy things all day.

I do what I see people do

and say just what they say.

BUS →

If Grover says,
"Hello, Big Bird.
Good morning,
how are you?"

then I will say,
"Hello, Big Bird.
Good morning,
how are you?"

I eat the same things
Cookie eats....

Well, maybe not quite all.

I hop the way

that Ernie hops

and try hard
not to fall.

I flap my wings
and peck and coo

like pigeons in the park.

And when I see

my favorite dog

I wag my tail and bark.

Every time I hear
a baby talk,

well, I go
"ga-ga-goo."

And when she
drinks her bottle

I drink a bottle too.

I like to

copy Oscar.

I know just
what to say.

21

When someone
comes to visit me,

I tell her,
"Go away."

I can hoot
just like an owl.

I can buzz
just like a bee.

25

And sometimes when

I'm all alone

I even copy me.

I see the Count is counting
all the stars up in the sky.

Because I am a copycat,

that is what I will try.

And when he says,
"It's time for bed.
Good night, Big Bird,
sleep tight...."

I nod my head
and smile and say,
"Good night, Big Bird,
sleep tight."

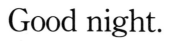

Good night.